T0353788

AuthorHouse™
1663 Liberty Drive
Bloomington, IN 47403
www.authorhouse.com
Phone: 1 (800) 839-8640

Published by AuthorHouse 12/31/2016

ISBN: 978-1-5246-5548-8 (sc)
ISBN: 978-1-5246-5689-8 (hc)
ISBN: 978-1-5246-5547-1 (e)

Library of Congress Control Number: 2016921123

Print information available on the last page.

This book is printed on acid-free paper.

authorHOUSE®

I-SPY and CANSEY and the Toy from the SKY

Twelve-pound Calico cat I-Spy and fifteen-pound Tuxedo cat Cansey wake up in the morning. Even though the sun is shining brightly through the window shade, it feels like just another day to them.

They eat.

They nap.

They jump onto the computer while Dad is trying to use it.

They wrestle. Cansey starts off with the upper hand as he gets a couple good swats in on I-Spy. He then leans back and stares intently and intensely at I-Spy to anticipate any countermove. He is ready for anything that I-Spy might try...

...except for when she sneezes in his face.

Despite the success of her unorthodox tactical maneuver, I-Spy feels no thrill. "I'm bored," she laments.

"Boredom sets into the boring mind," quips Cansey.

"Quiet, Big Brother! And what are you doing that's so exciting?"

"I'm being amused by you complaining."

"I can see you won't be any help. Wait. I know what the problem is. We need a new toy," says I-Spy.

"I-Spy, the last time Dad got you a new toy, it took you all of fifteen seconds to bat it under the couch where you couldn't reach it," says Cansey.

"So that means we don't need a new toy? If Dad would clean under the couch more often, we wouldn't run out of toys," retorts I-Spy.

"I'm saying if you were more careful, you wouldn't keep running out of toys."

"What's the point of that? Since when do mice always run in the direction most convenient for you? Dad just needs to clean more often."

"But in the meantime, here you are bored. How does that help us now?" points out Cansey.

I-Spy brightens. "I have an idea!"

"What is it?" asks Cansey.

"You know how people always say if you believe in something strongly enough, you can make it happen?"

"Yeah."

"Let's test it!" exclaims I-Spy.

"How?"

"I believe that if I go outside on the patio, a toy will fall from the sky and land in the yard so that we'll have a new toy to play with!" proclaims I-Spy.

Cansey barely chokes down a guffaw. "Well, with that attitude, it'll never happen," chastises I-Spy.

"I-Spy, it's good to have a positive attitude about things, but you have to balance that with being realistic. Under what possible circumstance could a toy fall out of the sky and land in our backyard? Do you think a pilot is going to open his door mid-flight, drop a toy, and calculate where it will land so perfectly that you'll get a new toy? All just for you?"

"I'm not saying I know exactly how it will happen. Besides, part of a positive attitude is being able to see the opportunity when it presents itself — even if it's not how you originally envisioned something happening."

"Okay. You go out onto the patio, and I'll watch.
This will be fun!" says Cansey.

Cansey foresees I-Spy sitting on the patio for hours upon hours staring at empty space while no toy comes to her. He savors the prospect of a good laugh at his sister's expense. Unfortunately for Cansey, his facial expression gives him away. "Big Brother, I'm not going to do this unless you make it worth my while. What are you going to do if I get a toy?"

"What do you want?"

I-Spy thinks about it for a second. "Fine. If I get a new toy, then you have to sleep on Dad's head tonight."

Cansey's confidence wavers just a fraction. He recovers quickly. "Okay. And if you don't get a new toy, then you have to sleep on Dad's head."

"Big Brother, since you seem so confident it won't happen, you get the entertainment of watching me. If you want something more, I'm just not going to do it."

"Okay. Okay. Fine," says Cansey hastily.

Meanwhile, Dad is in the kitchen making dinner. He regards his two cats facing each other with their paws tucked underneath their bodies. All of a sudden, I-Spy jumps up and makes a beeline for the patio door while Cansey stays put. Dad opens the patio door to let I-Spy outside feeling as mystified as ever by feline behavior.

I-Spy hears the door shut behind her. She looks back inside and sees her brother grinning from ear to ear. For a fleeting second, she considers caving in and conceding that Cansey was right. Then she pictures the satisfaction on his face. This gives her all the drive to succeed.

I-Spy stares up at a cloudless blue sky. In her mind's eye, she pictures a small round object moving across clear space and entering the backyard. She blocks out all other thoughts except this one image.

Five minutes pass. Ten minutes pass. Fifteen minutes pass.

Suddenly commotion occurs in the house next door. Someone next door is going outside into their backyard. I-Spy listens. It's a group of teenage boys. I-Spy listens further. It sounds like they're kicking something around among themselves. A few seconds later, I-Spy figures out what it is – a hacky sack! I-Spy gets excited. The possibility that she will be able to will her way to a new toy just became very real.

Meanwhile inside, Cansey could not hear the neighbor's door open or the boys step outside to play with their hacky sack. He just sees I-Spy sitting there looking as steadfastly hopeful as ever.

Cansey has to use the litter box. He decides that nothing will happen if he runs upstairs for a few minutes. He gets up from the living room to go upstairs.

Almost as if Cansey's resistant vibe was the last obstacle to be overcome, one of the boys boots the hacky sack...over the fence separating Dad's yard from the neighbor's yard. It falls out of the air and lands with a thud on the ground only a few feet from I-Spy.

For a few seconds, I-Spy is dazed herself. Maybe in her heart of hearts, I-Spy didn't really believe that she could will a toy out of the sky to land at her feet either. Yet there it is.

Recovering quickly, I-Spy picks up the hacky sack in her mouth and walks back to the patio door. Her claws scratching at the door inform Dad that she is ready to come in.

Dad dutifully opens the door for her, and I-Spy proudly trots in with her newly acquired toy. Dad does a double take when he sees the hacky sack in I-Spy's mouth.

At the exact same moment, Cansey steps off the bottom stair to turn back into the living room. He is expecting I-Spy to still be outside in her same position.

He sees I-Spy. He sees the hacky sack in her mouth. Cansey's eyes go as wide as saucers as he tries to process the information that his eyes have just sent to his brain.

I-Spy momentarily sets her toy on the floor. "You have to sleep on Dad's head tonight, Big Brother."

27

Cansey gulps. It never really occurred to him that I-Spy might actually get a toy from sitting in the backyard. He never fully contemplated the consequences of losing the bet. Now all he can think is that eight hours will seem like an eternity while he battles Dad as Dad tries to fall asleep. How will he get out of it?

To make matters worse, I-Spy decides that it would be appropriate to taunt her brother by playing with her new toy in front of him. She bats it back and forth, well away from any toy-swallowing furniture.

"Thanks for reminding me to play away from the couch, Big Brother. You're right. I can have more fun this way. It's something to pass the time until the fun tonight," says I-Spy to Cansey.

Cansey loses his temper. He leaps at I-Spy and tries to snatch the hacky sack away from her. He wasn't quick enough. I-Spy stabs the toy with her claw and pulls it away. "My idea, my toy!" she shouts.

Meanwhile, Dad observes I-Spy hiss at Cansey.
"Knock it off, you two!" Dad himself yells.

I-Spy and Cansey stop to look at Dad. Then they turn away. "You'll have to get Dad to get a toy out from under the couch, Big Brother," I-Spy says more calmly.

29

Cansey turns and runs away feeling defeated. He climbs the stairs, jumps onto the guest bed in the study, and curls up a ball.

Alone with his thoughts, Cansey sets about trying to figure a way out of his predicament. It takes about an hour, but something comes to mind. It's an idea that he likes. Then he pictures I-Spy accusing him of cheating. Cansey gets his response ready and vows not to lose his nerve if and when the time comes.

Meanwhile, downstairs, I-Spy grows tired of her new toy. She drops it against a wall for safekeeping. Then she heads upstairs herself to find Cansey. She jumps onto the bed next to him.

"I'm done with my toy, Big Brother. We can play if you want," she says.

"No. You were mean downstairs," says Cansey.

"I didn't mean it. You know that," responds I-Spy.

"No!"

I-Spy is a little taken aback. "Fine. Be petty like that," she says. She jumps off the bed. Just as she exits the room, she says back over to Cansey," You still have to honor your bet tonight, Big Brother."

"Whatever," retorts Cansey.

Cansey remains curled up in a ball on the guest bed for the entire evening. At 11:30 pm, Dad climbs into bed, turns out the light, and pulls the comforter up over his shoulder. I-Spy prances into the study.

"It's time, Big Brother. You can't lay there forever."

"I'm not going to try to sleep on Dad's head before he's fallen asleep. That will just make Dad grouchy and that's dumb," says Cansey.

"So you're backing out of your bet?"

"As you've often said to me, I-Spy, patience. Just wait until he falls asleep. You can let me know when that is."

"Big Brother –"

"You already won your bet and you get the entertainment value of watching what happens. If you want something more, I'm just not going to do it!" I-Spy feels proud of himself for being able to mimic I-Spy from earlier.

I-Spy takes the punch. "Fine, but you'd better not chicken out once Dad does fall asleep."

Tossing and turning from Dad follows. Dad seems to be having trouble getting comfortable. For one brief second, Cansey wonders if Dad will toss and turn all night so that he can get out of his bet. Then all is still.

"So what's your excuse this time?" mocks I-Spy.

Wordlessly, Cansey jumps off the guest bed, plods into the bedroom, and jumps up onto Dad's bed. I-Spy is now genuinely intrigued and follows. "If you wake Dad up, the bet's off!" warns Cansey.

"I won't say a word."

Cansey watches Dad carefully. Dad is sleeping like a log. Step by step, Cansey steadily inches closer to Dad's head. I-Spy knows that Cansey has some trick ready but cannot guess what it is.

Cansey is now close enough to breathe on Dad's face. Is he really going to try to sleep on Dad's head?

No, he isn't. Cansey carefully walks on the pillow around Dad's head before lying down. He curls himself around Dad's head like a pair of headphones. His fur is so close that it almost touches Dad's hair. Cansey's front paws rest a few inches from the left side of Dad's face. His rear paws rest a few inches from the right side of Dad's face. Cansey is sleeping around Dad's head.

In spite of herself, I-Spy wishes she had a camera to take a picture. Her brother and Dad both look so peaceful. She softens her stance. "Okay, Big Brother. Half an hour like that, and your bet is fulfilled."

The next morning, Dad wakes up feeling more rejuvenated than usual. He goes for a jog, showers, and sits down to breakfast. Even a knock at the front door in the middle of breakfast can't dampen his spirits.

I-Spy, on the other hand, darts up the stairs and crawls under the bed as is her habit whenever there is a knock at the front door. Cansey continues to rest downstairs.

Dad opens the front door. It's the boy from next door. "Sorry to bother you, Sir, but I kicked my hacky sack over the fence yesterday. Did you get it?"

In that moment, I-Spy realizes she left the hacky sack against the wall. She mentally kicks herself for not having grabbed it before running upstairs.

Meanwhile, Dad walks over to the wall to pick up the hacky sack. Cansey shoots Dad a look as if to say "What are you doing?" Dad barely registers Cansey's expression as he takes it to the boy.

"Thank you, Sir."

"You're welcome."

I-Spy storms back down the stairs. "Why didn't you grab it?" she complains to her brother.

"Well, it was his hacky sack," says Cansey.

I-Spy fumes as she cannot think up a good response. "So now what are we supposed to play with?"

"You could go outside and try to wish yourself another toy. I might even bet you again," says Cansey.

Before I-Spy can respond, Dad watches I-Spy and Cansey staring at each other. "Are you two unhappy that you lost your new toy?" he says. Dad pauses for a second. "Dad's going to give his kitties a treat." He picks up one side of the couch. Sure enough, two multicolored balls are resting underneath just out of paw's reach. I-Spy and Cansey get excited as Dad picks up the balls. "Dad just had an idea. He should've thought of this long ago."

Dad walks over to the patio door and opens it. Then he tosses the balls outside. I-Spy and Cansey comprehend immediately; they can't bat balls under the couch if they're outside.

I-Spy and Cansey charge through the open door and start batting
balls around carefree and to their hearts' content. Eventually,
they tire of their toys. The day has warmed up considerably,
and there is not a cloud in the sky on this day either.

It's the perfect day to luxuriate. I-Spy and Cansey trot to the middle of the
yard, roll over on their backs, and expose their bellies to the sunlight.

They have their toys. They have a good home. They have each
other, and they have beautiful weather. Life is good.

THE END.

Printed in the United States
By Bookmasters